The S of Tara

Waterford City and County Libraries

This story was adapted by author Ann Carroll
and illustrated by Derry Dillon

Published 2016
Poolbeg Press Ltd

123 Grange Hill, Baldoyle
Dublin 13, Ireland

Text © Poolbeg Press Ltd 2016

A catalogue record for this book is available from the British Library.

ISBN 978 1 78199 917 2

Cover design and illustrations by Derry Dillon
Printed by GPS Colour Graphics Ltd, Alexander Road, Belfast BT6 9HP

This book belongs to

- -

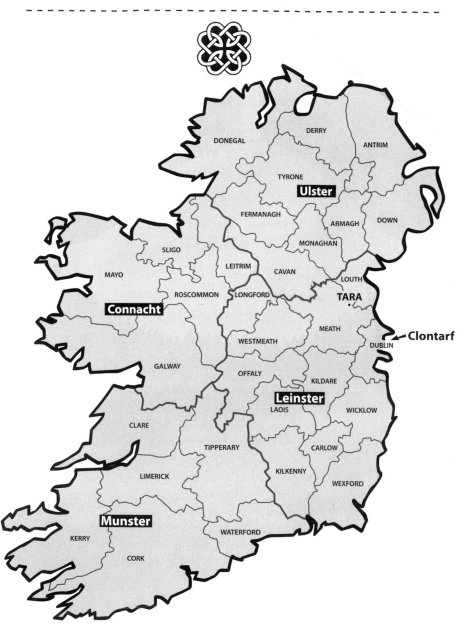

DONEGAL

DERRY

ANTRIM

TYRONE

Ulster

FERMANAGH

ARMAGH

DOWN

MONAGHAN

SLIGO

LEITRIM

CAVAN

MAYO

LOUTH

ROSCOMMON

LONGFORD

TARA

Connacht

MEATH

← **Clontarf**

WESTMEATH

DUBLIN

GALWAY

OFFALY

KILDARE

Leinster

LAOIS

WICKLOW

CLARE

TIPPERARY

CARLOW

LIMERICK

KILKENNY

WEXFORD

Munster

WATERFORD

KERRY

CORK

Also in the Nutshell series

The Tuatha Dé Danann

Long, long ago they arrived in Ireland.

Huge clouds thundered through the sky and touched the land. Darkness came for three days. The clouds lifted at last, leaving behind a great tribe, known as the Tuatha Dé Danann, the People of the Goddess Danu.

One of the treasures they brought with them was a huge magical stone and this they stood on the Hill of Tara.

In time the Tuatha Dé Danann decided their stay on earth was over and went to live underground. Here they became the Immortals – pagan gods who lived in the Other World and who kept an eye on everything in this one.

Their gift, the great standing stone, can still be seen on Tara's hill.

The Stone Age People

Casla was only eleven when his father, as leader of the tribe, decided they should settle in the valley.

Part of a Stone Age group, arriving around 3000 BC long after the time of Tuatha Dé Danann, they were ready to leave their own mark on Tara.

"This is your chance to prove yourself!" Casla's father told him.

Casla was eager to show his strength. "I already know how to make daggers and sharp flint heads for axe and spear. I'll help clear the forest and build the wooden houses."

His father smiled. "You are a good son, nearly a man now. It's time for you to hunt deer and wild boar deep in the forest."

The boy caught his breath. Nearly a man now! He knew how exciting and dangerous a man's life could be – and he couldn't wait.

Soon after their arrival, on a clear summer's day, the group climbed to the top of the Hill of Tara.

"A good look-out," said Casla's father. "We can see far away and in every direction."

"And it's an excellent place for our dead," added one of the elders. He pointed at the standing stone. "This stone will guard them. It belongs to the gods and has their magic."

So Casla helped build a passage tomb into the hilltop at Tara. Inside the entrance the best sculptors carved a stone with wonderful decorations.

Around the tomb they built a huge circle of wooden pillars.

These look like a giant army against the sky, Casla thought.

When his father died, Casla was nearly twenty. The funeral pyre was placed on the hill and the body burned for three days. Then the ashes were placed in the passage tomb.

Later Casla would have the same funeral but not until he had taken his father's place and been a good leader for a long time.

Over the next 1500 years burials were held. The remains of more than 200 people were placed in the tomb. Often gifts were put into urns over the ashes: things people had used in life, such as necklaces, battle-axes, bone pins, flint knives – all went with them to the After-life.

During this time people who knew how to make a metal called bronze came to Ireland, and after that bronze weapons and tools were also buried in the passage grave.

The Stone Age was over.

The Bronze Age Boy

He was only fourteen when he died. He must have been important, for he wore a precious necklace, made from amber, jet, bronze and faience.

Maybe he'd been a boy of promise, good at hunting, swift and strong. No one knows how he died, only that his body wasn't burnt, but carefully laid in the tomb sometime during the Bronze Age, about 4000 years ago.

Perhaps the necklace was meant to show the gods how well the boy had been regarded and how much he'd been loved.

The Iron Age

Around 500 BC a new people arrived in
Ireland from Europe. These were the Celts.
They were very powerful because they had a
huge advantage over the Bronze Age people.
They knew how to make iron and their weapons
were much stronger than bronze ones. Soon
their language and way of life had spread all
over Ireland.

At this time each area in Ireland had a local king and often there were rows and battles. Then the time came when people began to wish there was one overall leader who could bring peace.

The Stone of Destiny

The people met at Tara and decided they would call this leader the High King.

One man stepped forward, put his hand on the magical standing stone, and said, "I am the bravest warrior and will rule wisely if you choose me to be High King."

They set him a number of challenges to prove his strength and wisdom, all of which he successfully met.

Then he stood again at the standing stone, placed his hand on it and told the huge crowd: "I am your High King!"

Before anyone could say a word, the stone shrieked with immense power and the eerie sound was heard in all corners of Ireland.

The people stepped back in fear, but the new High King said: "This is the Lia Fáil, the Stone of Destiny. From now on, whoever wants to be High King must meet with the Stone's approval."

And so it happened through all the centuries of High Kings that followed: no candidate was successful unless the Stone of Destiny shrieked and was heard throughout the land.

Cormac Mac Airt

Four of the 142 kings who ruled from Tara are special, because they held power at important times.

The first of these was Cormac Mac Airt.

He brought a great Band of Warriors, the Fianna, to Tara. There they protected the High King against all enemies.

Among them was Fionn Mac Cumhaill, the hero who killed a fire-breathing spirit, Aillen.

Every year Aillen's spell put the warriors at Tara into a deep sleep. Then he burnt Cormac's palace down.

When Fionn came, he made sure to stay awake by prodding his forehead with his spear so that he couldn't nod off with the pain. Then he rid Tara of the evil spirit forever.

Cormac was High King for forty years and he had the first great army in Ireland.

Laoghaire

The second great king was Laoghaire, High King when Saint Patrick brought Christianity to Ireland.

Laoghaire believed in Paganism and each year, at Imbolc or the Rites of Spring, he lit a huge bonfire on the Hill of Tara. This was to encourage the gods to bring growth to the land.

No one else was allowed to have a fire on that day under pain of death, but Patrick lit a huge bonfire at nearby Slane as a challenge.

When Laoghaire saw this, he and his followers marched on Slane and the High King vowed, "The man who has defied me will die!"

However, when he met Patrick he was impressed and invited him to Tara. They talked for a long time and finally Laoghaire said, "You have my permission to tell any who will listen about your god."

He himself kept to the old ways and when he died he was buried upright at Tara, holding a spear, ready for his enemies.

After a while the people stopped believing in the old gods. Heaven replaced the Other World and Christianity replaced Paganism.

Brian Boru

The third special High King was Brian Boru, said to be the greatest of all.

A brave warrior and a great leader, the Vikings were his sworn enemy.

These first came in their longboats from Norway, Sweden and Denmark in the 10th century, bringing death and grief.

But they met their match in Brian, who defeated them in battle after battle.

Then Sitric, one of the beaten Vikings, joined forces with Mael Morda, who hated the High King.

"The Vikings on Orkney and the Isle of Man are my friends. They'll help us," Sitric said.

So they gathered a great army at Clontarf. Brian met them with his warriors and on Good Friday 1014 the battle began.

At one point Brian went to his tent to rest and pray for victory. While he was on his knees, the Viking, Brodir, sneaked in and killed him.

The Irish were so furious they fought even more fiercely, winning the battle and killing most of the enemy.

It was a great turning point, and afterwards the Vikings who remained in Ireland settled down to lasting peace.

Ruairí Ó Conchobhair

In 1166 Ruairí was High King when Tiernan Ó Ruairc, King of Breifne, came to him at Tara.

"You must help me!" Tiernan told him. "Diarmuid Mac Murchadha has stolen my wife and he's not fit to be King of Leinster!"

Together they marched on Leinster and drove Diarmuid away to England.

At that time the Normans were ruling England and Diarmuid got the help of one Norman leader Richard de Clare, later known as Strongbow.

His army arrived in 1170 and captured Waterford and Dublin. Later he married Diarmuid's daughter, Aoife.

Those who came with Strongbow never went back. Later, others followed, and Ireland came under English rule for centuries.

And it all began when Ruairí was High King.

The Battle of Tara: 1798

In time there were no more High Kings, but Tara remained important to the Irish.

One of the battles the United Irishmen fought against the English took place at Tara in May 1798.

Fifteen-year-old Conor was among the 4000 rebels who gathered there.

"What do you think, Henry? Will we beat them?" he asked his older brother.

"How could we not beat them?" Henry replied. "All we have to do is remember the Fianna. We know how brave they were!"

But soon Conor knew courage wasn't enough. The King's soldiers swarmed up the hill on foot and horseback, firing muskets. The rebels, with their pikes and pitchforks, hardly got near them.

Canon was loaded and wave after wave of rebels were killed. Conor saw Henry fall as the air became thick with smoke.

He stumbled over and knelt by his side.

"We have no chance," Henry gasped. "You must save yourself!"

"Run away?"

"Stay alive."

Henry had a dreadful wound in his neck and Conor held him till he'd stopped breathing. Then he lay down by his brother and let the battle rage. As soon as it was dark he slipped down the hillside and escaped.

Four hundred rebels died that day and were buried on the hill.

To honour their death the Lia Fáil was moved to mark their grave.

The Monster Meeting at Tara

Seven-year-old Josie sat on her father's shoulders as he strode along the road to Tara. It was August 15th 1843 and they were two among thousands.

"What's Mister O'Connell going to tell us, Da?" Josie asked.

"That we should be ruled by the Irish and that Irish laws should be passed here, not in England! It's a great day for Ireland and I want you to be there to hear Daniel O'Connell speak at one of his Monster Meetings!"

Josie had one worry. "Will there be monsters, Da?"

"Not a one. But there'll be a quarter of a million people, so that's a monster crowd. And all here to listen to the great man."

They had to stop a good distance from the hill, unable to get closer. Luckily they could see Daniel O'Connell on the hilltop but Josie couldn't hear a word and went to sleep, her head slumped over her father's.

Afterwards everyone was in great form as they marched home, telling each other over and over that it was a great day for Ireland.

But O'Connell's plan failed. Instead he was arrested and spent three months in prison. Four years later, suffering from bad health, he went to Italy where he died.

But even when she was an old lady of eighty, Josie remembered the day as one of great happiness.

Last Word

In 2010 the M3 motorway was opened 2.3 kilometres away from Tara. Many fear it is too close, disturbing the site with roadworks and heavy traffic. And who knows what treasures might still be buried around the area?

So there is another battle to fight for Tara. Hopefully this one will be successful, for it is an amazing place.

The End

Word Sounds

(Opinions may differ regarding pronunciation)

Words	Sounds
Tuatha Dé Danaan	Too-aha Day Dan-an
Celts	Kelts
Mac Airt	Mock Art
Lia Fáil	Lee-ah Faw-yil
Aillen	Aw-lin
Fionn Mac Cumhaill	Fee-un Mock Cool
Laoghaire	Lay-ra
Imbolc	Imbolg
Boru	Boroo
Sitric	Sitrick
Mael Morda	Male More-da
Brodir	Bro-deer
Ruairí Ó Conchobhair	Roo-ary O Cruh-hoor
Tiernan Ó Ruairc	Teer-nan O Roo-ark
Diarmuid	Deer-mid
Mac Murchadha	Mock Mur-aha
Aoife	Ee-fa
Fianna	Fee-ana